AVA
A Story of Friendship

Marianne Shrader

For my Grandchildren

.

Once you have had a wonderful dog,
a life without one is a life diminished

Dean Koontz, author

CONTENTS

ACKNOWLEDGMENTS

Special thanks go to my family, my husband, Steve, my boys, Ed and Phil and my sisters, Dr. Eva Ettedgui and Lya Grote, who have encouraged me to write. I appreciate input that I received from my nephew, Emile Ettedgui, and my little friend Zack Hayes who critiqued my story from a nine year old's perspective.

CHAPTER I

THE WALK TO GRANDMA'S

Tall trees along the sidewalk dressed in spring's light green finery stood at attention as Ava walked past with her head held high. The gentle west wind caressed her face and overhead the sun showered her with golden rays from the sky. Pink and yellow flowers that recently popped their heads from the ground smiled at her. It seemed as if the whole world knew how happy she was. And, indeed, she was happier than she ever had been in all her life.

Pausing at the base of a large elm tree she stopped to sniff the scents on the ground and almost jumped out of her skin with delight. She relished the moment. Life was good. A gentle tug on her leash got her going again. It was a signal to move on and keep the sniffing to a minimum. Ah, it would have been nice to linger and savor the aroma around the tree. But move on she did.

It was Dad who was holding the other end of her leash. He was the best thing that had ever happened to her in her short life. She had been on lots of walks with him and was familiar with the routes they usually took, but today was different. Not only were they on a street unknown to her but Dad wasn't strolling as was his habit. He was moving quickly and with a purpose. In addition Dad's three children had come along. Most of the time the walks only included Ava and Dad.

Ava wanted to take her time and check out each tree and blade of grass but Dad wasn't giving her the chance.

"Come on, Ava," he said. "We're taking you to meet Grandma."

Ava had no idea who Grandma was but she was content to go anywhere with Dad when a strong, fresh scent hit her nose. It was nice. She was curious to know what it was. By instinct she moved her head from side to side and up and down, sniffing all the while. It was coming from the right so she headed in that direction crossing in front of Dad. She found it stronger in the air than on the ground and even more so when she held her nose between the slats of the wooden fence that they were passing. The opening between the boards was too small for her to see what was on the other side but there was no denying the presence of another four legged creature. Suddenly it began barking with an irritating high pitch and frantically running back and forth along the fence line. He sounded as if he was afraid for his life and wanted to protect himself and his yard from these foreign intruders.

Ava stood mute. Her interest was solely his smell which was enticing. She didn't care a hoot about him otherwise. Then scratching the soil with her rear legs and taking another sniff of the air, Ava snorted. Dad understood this as an act of aggression.

"Let's not have a confrontation, with the little fellow." said Dad. "You be a good girl, Ava, and come along."

Ava obeyed Dad because she worshipped him and wanted to do everything to please him. But she was ready to move on anyway. Holding her head high she walked past the fence as if that dog on the other side didn't exist.

Ava had not been living with Dad for very long. She came to his home from a shelter where she had lived for the entire two years of her life. Many dogs lived in the shelter, some longer than others, and all of them waited patiently to someday be adopted by a human family.

The adoption step was simple. A person who wanted a pet came to the shelter, and was introduced to three dogs. He then spent some time alone with each dog so they could get to know each other. If he liked one of the dogs he took him home. But, if none of the dogs appealed to him, the visitor could come back another time and go through this process again with three new dogs. There was no limit to these doggie interviews but usually the visitor found the perfect pet for his family after one or two times at the shelter.

Ava had experienced these sessions but had never been picked by anyone. She liked some of the people that she had met but didn't have a special warm feeling toward any of them. And, evidently, they didn't toward her either because no one had ever wanted her.

Before she met Dad the shelter was the only life that she had ever known. And Ava was content to stay there. She didn't know that she was missing out on anything by not being adopted. Sometimes, though, she did wonder what life was like elsewhere. She knew of only one dog that had been returned where the adoption didn't work out but all other dogs were permanently placed and they didn't come back. There was no way to know how they fit into their new homes. It was safe to assume that they were happy, but Ava would never know for sure.

It was on a cold and windy day early in March that she first met Dad. From then on her life took a sudden change. He had come to the shelter to adopt a dog. Ava and two others were introduced to him. When Ava saw Dad and heard his voice a warm tingle rushed through her body. She had a sudden urge to be close to him. But she was dog number three and she had to wait while Dad spent time with dog one and dog two before she could have her time alone with him. She had never felt like this with anyone before and she truly wished to become his pet.

When it was her turn to be with Dad, Ava's heart was beating so fast it looked like it would pop through her ribcage. She went up to him and tried to climb into his lap, but he told her she had to stay down. Ava wanted Dad to like her as much as she liked him and when he spoke to her, she swooned.

After the visit, Dad patted her on her head, said some nice things and started to leave. Ava wanted to follow him but one of the caretakers stopped her.

"You can't go with him," he said. "You have to stay here. Come," he added, "we'll go play in the yard."

Ava wasn't interested in playing but did follow the caretaker. She felt alone and rejected. Outside she had no interest in doing anything. She lay on the ground, put her head down and brooded.

From the moment Dad left, her life took a turn. She was lost, lonely and sad at the same time, new emotions she had never experienced in the past.

Nothing seemed to interest her. In the yard one of the caretakers whistled to get her attention. She had a ball in her hand. Ava glanced toward her but didn't move. The caretaker tossed it away from them in the yard.

"Fetch, Ava, fetch," she called.

But Ava didn't budge. She wanted nothing to do with it and ignored the caretaker.

Later during dinner hour, Ava went inside and found her food in her special dish. She sniffed it, picked at it and ate some of it. She wasn't hungry.

A few days after Dad's visit, Ava was moping in the side yard when she heard the chugging of a motor. She looked up, more out of curiosity than anything else because the noise was irritating. Pulling into the driveway was a blue pickup truck. Her heart skipped a beat when she saw Dad step out of it. There were three children with him and they were walking toward the front door.

Ava sat up and watched but Dad didn't notice her nor did he even look her way. He just went straight into the shelter. Dropping her head to the ground Ava was ready to cry, her heart completely broken. The intense happiness she felt when she met Dad was compounded with utter loneliness when he left without her. Now he was back so she could re-live the pain of being separated from him.

A short time later, which seemed like an eternity, Ava thought she heard someone call her name. She did not move but kept her head close to the ground as she wallowed in her misery. Then she heard her name again. This time she lifted her head and looked in the direction of the voice. There was Dad, bigger than life, and he was walking toward her. Confusion filled her mind. She didn't understand what was happening but she heard Dad's voice which was music to her ears.

"You're coming home with us, Ava," said Dad. "You will be part of our family."

Ava didn't understand a word he was saying but his presence and his tone told it all. There is no way to the adequately describe the intense joy that passed through Ava's body. She jumped two feet off the ground, then turned in circles and whined to demonstrate her happiness. She wanted to hug Dad and did so as best as she could. She put her paws on his chest and nuzzled her head in the crook of his arm. She felt the warmth of his body radiate into her own and she was happy.

When Ava settled down, Dad laughed and introduced his children. Cody was the oldest. He was in high school and he was almost as tall as Dad. Amanda was next. She had long dark hair and big brown eyes. She was in middle school and was very quiet but very pretty. The third child was Lindsey. She had light brown hair and was still in elementary school. She looked like a little tomboy but she was pretty too.

Cody and Lindsey hugged Ava around the neck. They were so happy to have a new addition to the family.

Amanda simply stared at her. "She's kind of ugly, Dad. Do we really want her?"

Dad didn't say anything but gave a look to Amanda that meant she shouldn't say such things.

Amanda shrugged her shoulders then patted Ava's head. "OK, you're fine," she said. "We can take you home."

Ava could not believe how lucky she was to be adopted by such a wonderful family. This feeling of joy had not left her since she moved into Dad's home and today the whole family was out walking her.

Ava moved forward and stopped to smell the base of a small tree. She managed to wrap the leash around the trunk so she couldn't move.

Dad freed the leash then continued to walk at his same pace. He was anxious to get to Grandma's. Ava, on the other hand, wanted to study each spot they passed. Dad did not give her the chance to do so.

*   *   *

CHAPTER II

MEETING GRANDMA

Dad turned into a driveway and led everyone through a gate to a fenced in yard. When they were all inside and the gate closed, Dad removed the leash from Ava's collar and she was free to roam and explore on her own. Ava looked around and was stunned at the sight of grey everywhere. There was no grass in this small yard. The whole area was covered with patio stones with just a small patch of dirt around the edges. Ava sniffed here and sniffed there. She held her nose close to the ground but the stones had no smell. There was nothing enticing about this yard. As she approached the fence with her nose glued to the ground, she reached the small strip of soil. Here was something that she liked, dirt and odors. That was more like it. At one time, other dogs had been here before her. She lay down to roll around in that little strip but only her shoulders fit on the dirt. The rest of her body was on patio stones. It wasn't an ideal situation.

Opposite to where Ava was rolling on the ground was a big house. Dad went up to the door and rang the bell. A few seconds later a lady stepped outside and gave Dad and each of the children a kiss and a hug.

Dad called Ava over. "I want you to meet Grandma." He indicated the lady. Then turning to Grandma he said, "This is Ava."

Ava ran over to greet her "dog fashion" with a good sniff. When she pushed her nose up to Grandma's hand, Grandma jerked it away.

On seeing this Cody said, "Don't you like her, Grandma?"

"It's not that I don't like her," answered Grandma. "I need some time to get to know her. She's a very large dog and, besides, her nose is wet." And she stepped back to make the distance between her and the dog greater.

And indeed Ava's nose was very wet and she was big. She was a pit bull. The name itself evoked fear in people and being face to face with one was even more unnerving. These dogs were used for dog fights and they had a reputation of being vicious. Yes, Grandma was uncomfortable. Had Dad not been there we could say she would have been scared.

When Dad was thinking of adopting Ava he had told Grandma that Pit Bulls are really nice and friendly dogs. "They are good with people but they only get aggressive with other dogs," he said.

Grandma wanted to believe that but looking at Ava and seeing her strong frame she could not. She had a hard time believing Dad and she was not relaxed with Ava.

Who knew what movement or sound would trigger this dog to attack. Grandma stepped slowly and spoke in quiet and gentle tones. She had never personally met a Pit Bull in her life and was going to tread with caution as far as this dog was concerned.

"Maybe when I get to know her a little better," continued Grandma, "I'll be more relaxed in her company." She looked at Cody. Then not to disappoint him that she wasn't overly fond of his dog she continued. "Actually, I'm that way with people also. It takes me a while to warm up to someone that I don't know."

Grandma was nervous and deep down doubted if she would ever feel comfortable in this dog's presence. She worried about the safety of Dad's children and never took her eyes off Ava.

She went on talking as if to herself. "My grandmother loved dogs but she always told me to be careful and cautious with strange dogs." Then pausing a moment, she leaned toward Cody and spoke directly into his ear, "especially Pit Bulls." She smiled and backed away. "You never know how they'll react if they don't know you. I always listened to everything that my Grandmother said."

"Everything?" asked Cody.

Grandma laughed. "Everything," she repeated. But she thought to herself, *not really*. When Grandma was a child she was terrified of dogs. As a little girl whenever she saw a dog she ran for her life even though her grandmother had told her never to do that. She had said that if you run, a dog will think you want to play. He will instinctively chase anything that moves. But as a little girl Grandma was not convinced and took off as fast as she could if she ever sighted a dog. And they always did chase her and scare her.

Meanwhile Ava's attention was directed to further exploring the soil in the yard, what little there was of it. Ava was enjoying the smells. If only they hadn't put those darn patio stones down, she could get a better scent of what and who had been there before. She paid no attention to anyone around her until she heard Dad's voice.

"Shall we introduce Ava to Gigi and Cuppa?"

Cuppa was how they called their Grandpa. Gigi was Grandma's mother and great-grandma to Dad's children. She lived in the house with Grandma and Cuppa and she was very old.

"I don't know how Gigi will respond to her and I don't know how your dog will behave in the house," said Grandma.

"She'll be fine," assured Dad. Cody, Amanda and Lindsey weren't interested in all the introductions and ran downstairs to Grandma's basement where there was a family room for the children.

Dad called to Ava to come and they went into the house. Grandma followed slowly behind. Inside they found Cuppa standing in the hallway at the foot of the stairs.

"Hello, Ava," he said. "I'm so happy to meet you." He rubbed the top of her head. "I've heard so much about you," he added. Ava wagged her tail and got close to Cuppa.

Dad then led Ava into another room where a white haired lady was sitting in an easy chair watching television. It was Gigi. Gigi was over ninety years old and used a walker to get around. She claimed the TV room as her territory and everyone had to watch what she selected on the TV. Gigi had known that Dad got a Pit Bull for a pet and she had already told both Grandma and Dad that she didn't want "that dog" anywhere near her. Now they were bringing "that dog" into the house and the TV room where she spent so much of her time.

When Gigi looked up and saw Ava coming toward her, she started screaming.

"I don't want 'that dog' here. I don't like her. She's ugly and looks mean." She held her hands in front of her to protect herself.

Ava stopped in her tracks, turned and ran back into the kitchen. She was scared of Gigi and hurt. She held her head low and lay down on the kitchen floor while she waited for Dad to come back.

"Ava," said Dad as he walked calmly into the kitchen. "It will be all right. Gigi didn't mean all that she said. She will learn to like you. You'll see. You will be staying here at Grandma's while we go away for Spring

Break and then you and Grandma and Gigi can become friends."

On the way home Ava hung her head low. She could not get excited about any of the smells by the sidewalk. It seemed that the trees barely noticed her as she passed by and the flowers drooped their heads. The gentle breeze didn't caress her face and the sun was hiding behind a cloud. The meeting at Grandma's was a disaster.

*   *   *

CHAPTER III

SPRING BREAK

The introduction to the extended family at Grandma's was soon forgotten and life continued on an even keel until one morning a couple of weeks after. Ava had eaten her breakfast and was resting comfortably after her morning walk with Dad when she noticed that something was different. Dad was packing her toys and pillow into a plastic bag. Next he took her kennel, a large cage in which Ava slept during the night, and folded it up. Ava watched quietly. There were changes happening and they made Ava uneasy. She kept a steady eye on Dad.

Dad glanced at her and as if sensing her question said, "I'm taking you to Grandma's." He patted her on the head. "It's Spring Break and the kids and I will be gone for a few days. Grandma will take good care of you."

The word "Grandma" brought back visions of that fateful day when she met Dad's family. Ava shuddered. She didn't really understand everything that Dad was saying but she had bad vibes about what was going on around her. Dad's movements and motions were not part of their usual routine and she didn't like it.

Dad took her things and loaded them into his truck. He then came to get her. When he clipped the leash to her collar, Ava sensed that they were not going for a walk. She moved cautiously. Dad took her outside and opened the door to the truck.

"Up and inside," he said.

Ava jumped in still confused as to what was happening. She watched out the window and recognized the way to Grandma's house. When Dad pulled into the driveway Ava was not happy. She took her time getting out of the truck then moved slower than a snail. Dad pulled her leash but she refused to go any faster. Inside Grandma's yard Ava sniffed a few times but, for the most part, wasn't interested in what was there or what had been there at any one time. She kept her eyes on Dad and followed him with every move he took.

Dad unloaded the kennel and all her things and brought them into the house. He then set up the kennel on the floor in Grandma's dining room and put his hand on Ava's head. "I want you to be a very good dog while we are away and do as Grandma says."

He rubbed her chin and gave her a big hug. Although Dad's hug felt warm and loving, Ava sensed that something was wrong. She was apprehensive and followed close behind Dad as he walked out of the house and into the yard. When he opened the gate she was ready to leave with him but told her to stay. He closed the gate behind him. Ava stood by the fence and cried as she watched him get into the truck and drive away.

*   *   *.

CHAPTER IV

GRANDMA BEFRIENDS AVA

Grandma stood by the back door and waved to Dad as he was leaving. She wasn't crying like Ava but she wasn't happy either. Here was this dog that she didn't know and it was taking up temporary residence in her home. She didn't want to admit that she was afraid of Ava but she was. And she was scared of being alone with her. She wished that Cuppa was home to help her because he didn't mind the dog and had been comfortable with her. But, even though it was Saturday, he had to go to work to finish a project before he went out of town on a business trip early Monday morning. A cold shudder went through Grandma's body when she thought of the upcoming week.

As she stood on the back porch watching the dog Grandma felt her heart racing. She was scared. It was unnerving to be alone with this frightening creature. She didn't know how Ava would behave with Dad not around. The dog obeyed Dad and did everything he told her to do but how would she be with Grandma?

Taking a deep breath she stepped down onto the patio to address the dog. "Come inside," she said as softly and gently as she could. There was a tremor in her voice which she couldn't conceal. She hoped the dog did not sense her fear.

But Ava didn't care. She ignored Grandma, not moving from the fence nor even turning to let Grandma know she had heard her voice. Although she quit crying she held her eyes toward the driveway hoping Dad would come back. She heard Grandma calling her again but Ava stood her ground. Dad had left her. Actually he abandoned her with this strange woman in this strange house. She was broken hearted and not about to obey the woman they called Grandma.

Grandma tried to take control. She was entrusted with the care of this Pit Bull and she had to make the best of it. It was a temporary arrangement and a favor for Dad. She would do anything for him. So if Dad loved Ava, then Grandma would too, eventually. She didn't know how long it would take, but she would try very hard. She was hoping that this will work out well.

Cautiously she took a few steps closer to the dog then stopped.

"Come, Ava," she said.

There was no response. Grandma took a deep breath then trying to keep her voice as calm as possible under the circumstances she said, "Your Dad will be back in a few days."

It didn't matter what she said. Ava ignored her and was acting like a child who is left with a new baby sitter. But Ava was a dog and Grandma didn't know how to handle her. A child could be picked up and consoled but what do you do with a dog. She was too big to be held and Grandma wasn't too sure about getting close to her.

You can make friends with a kid and calm him by giving him a chocolate chip cookie but what do you do with a dog?

Grandma was at her wit's end. So she again started talking. "Dad will be back. He loves you and he just wants you to stay here because he can't take you on Spring Break."

Ava momentarily quit crying. Grandma breathed easier. Talking to Ava helped calm her own fears and she hoped it had a good effect on Ava. But Ava still didn't budge. There was no way of knowing what she thought.

Grandma's biggest fear was that Ava will bark at her or worse yet to growl at her. She didn't know what she would do in that case. Taking a couple more steps closer to Ava Grandma continued talking then froze when Ava turned her head and looked at her. Grandma's breath stopped and her heart beat faster. Her mouth went dry. There wasn't any spit in it when she tried to swallow. She expected Ava to bare her teeth but Ava turned her head back toward the driveway as if Grandma didn't exist. Again she began crying.

Taking a few steps closer to Ava, Grandma continued talking. "Grandma will take good care of you and Dad will be back. It's only for a few days. You'll see." She wanted to make sure that Ava knew she was coming closer to her. She didn't want to come up behind her and surprise her. That could be a dangerous situation, according to her grandmother. It was important to let the dog know that you are coming. *Keep talking so she is aware of your presence.*

When she got right up to Ava, Grandma wanted to touch her but was afraid. She continued with the soothing words until Ava stopped crying. Grandma then felt brave enough to place her hand gently on Ava's back. Feeling the warmth of Grandma's hand, Ava turned and looked up at Grandma. Her big brown eyes were filled with sadness and appeared to be swimming in a pool of tears. Grandma felt a pang in her heart and was sorry for the dog. She saw in Ava's eyes a warm and innocent creature in need of love. All her fears of Pit Bulls flew off into the distance. Her heart went out to this dog whose outside appearance was so different from what was inside her.

"We'll love you and treat you well, little dog," said Grandma her eyes also filling with tears. "I've looked into your heart and I like what I see. We'll get to know each other really well by the time Dad gets home. You'll see. We'll be good friends."

Grandma's words and the warmth of her hand did have a soothing effect on Ava. So when Grandma told her to come into the house, she slowly shuffled in. Grandma sat down by the kitchen table and Ava got comfortable by her feet.

"Let's stay in here, though, for now," said Grandma. "It might take Gigi a bit longer to make friends with you." She sighed then continued. "Life can be very difficult. Sometimes things happen to us and around us over which we have no control. People have a tendency to judge us by our appearance as I also judged you. Sometimes we have a chance to show those people that what they think about us is wrong but many times we don't get that chance. Unfortunately you look pretty scary and Pit Bulls do have a bad reputation, but I see that I was so wrong. I am sorry."

Ava didn't move. She didn't know what Grandma was talking about but was soothed by her tone. She also began to feel at ease in her company.

*   *   *

CHAPTER V

A WALK WITH GRANDMA

L ooking out the kitchen window and seeing the sun shining brightly Grandma longed to be outside. She called to Gigi from the doorway.

"I'll be gone for a little while. I'm taking Ava for a walk," she shouted.

Ava was transformed when she heard the word WALK. It was as if an arrow of energy shot into her. She jumped up, whined for joy then ran around in circles.

"Good grief. Settle down," said Grandma. "You don't have to get so excited."

But Ava would not be calm. Grandma could hardly clip the leash to her collar and when she opened the back door she had to grab the handrail so Ava wouldn't pull her down the stairs.

Outside Grandma took her in a direction where she had never been with either Dad or Cody. The path was unfamiliar and so were the scents. Ava forgot about her cares and troubles and enjoyed the new scenery, the chirping of birds and the light breeze in her face.

As they strolled along the sidewalk a man and woman coming toward them casually crossed the street before getting too near and continued on their way on the other side. Grandma then saw a lady in the near distance walking in their direction who also seemed to avoid them by crossing the street before she came close. Not long after, a group of teenagers was visible up ahead laughing and singing and jovially pushing each other. But when they spotted Ava, they also moved quickly, or so it seemed, to avoid them. It became continuous with whoever was out walking.

"It appears that people are making a point of not coming near us. They must be afraid of you, Puppy," said Grandma. "I hope you behave yourself with strangers and act as nicely as you have toward me."

But Grandma didn't have to worry about Ava acting up because no one passed them and no one came near them. Everyone crossed the street before they got close.

Ava didn't notice any of these people. She was intent on exploring what was on the ground, smelling everything they passed. Grandma wanted to walk briskly but Ava stalled. She wandered along stopping here and there. Grandma pulled on her leash to get her to move faster, but Ava held her ground doing what she wanted. So, on they went. It was peaceful and quiet until they were nearing a house where a woman was gardening in her front yard.

The yard was deep and the lady was near the house, a good distance from the sidewalk. When she looked up and saw Ava she didn't get up and leave or take refuge in her house. She continued with what she was doing but her little dog who was sitting next to her went ballistic. On seeing Ava he barked up a storm but stayed close to his owner. It looked like he was telling Ava to get lost and not to come near. Ava stiffened then snorted. Grandma also stiffened. The dog was not on a leash. He could decide to come at them. Then Dad's words flashed through her mind: *stay away from other dogs. Ava doesn't like them and will snap at them.* Grandma had visions of Ava devouring it in one bite. It was so small.

With soothing words she hoped to keep Ava calm and held the leash as tightly as she could, wrapping it several times around her wrist. She maintained her pace pulling Ava to follow her. Ava kept up with Grandma but she never took her eyes off that dog.

"Let's go, Ava. I want to get out of here," said Grandma and she began to walk faster. Ava felt the urgency and followed.

When directly in front of the yard, Grandma picked up her pace and began running. No sooner did she get her legs moving when the little dog bolted out toward them. Her Grandmother's wise words from her childhood flashed thorough her mind. *Don't run when you see a dog. He will follow you.* But just as she didn't heed these instructions then, she didn't now. All she wanted was to get away as fast and far away as she could. Grandma was sure that she and Ava could outrun him before he got to the sidewalk. But why didn't his owner stop him? The lady kept on with her gardening as if nothing was happening.

Grandma felt her heart in her throat. It was beating double time and her legs felt like they were made of lead. But she moved on. Her only comfort was that Ava kept pace with her. She started saying soothing words so Ava stayed calm. They seemed to have worked earlier for both Ava and her.

Grandma looked over her shoulder. They were almost past the yard but the little dog was almost to the sidewalk.

"Get back!" screamed Grandma. So much for soothing words. But Ava was not affected.

"It's all right. He's friendly," called the lady in the yard as she waved her hand in a hello.

"But mine's not," shouted Grandma and she kept running.

What the lady did or said to her dog after that Grandma didn't know nor did she care. She didn't stop to look back and didn't stop running until they turned the corner and the lady and her dog were safely out of sight. Then and only then did Grandma slow down and stop. She was panting, glad that nothing bad had happened. Ava's tongue was hanging out of her mouth and she was breathing heavily. She was ready to stop.

"I did not like that," said Grandma, trying to catch her breath between words. "People are not supposed to let their dogs out without a leash."

Ava didn't like it either. Running was not one of her favorite pastimes. And she let Grandma know. She sprawled out on the sidewalk and didn't get up until she was good and ready. No coaxing from Grandma could get her to move.

A good five minutes later and not until she was well rested did Ava get up and start walking. Grandma was frustrated, both with Ava and the walk. She now kept her eyes wide open ready to cross the street or go another way if she saw any dogs even if they were on a leash being walked by a human. She wasn't ready to test Ava's social skills with creatures of the four legged variety.

After they got home Grandma needed a rest. The walk that was supposed to be a pleasant way to spend an hour out of doors turned out to be a disaster. She was exhausted.

She headed to the TV room which was the best place in the house to nap. But that's where Gigi was and where she was watching TV.

"We now have to face another obstacle, Puppy," said Grandma turning to Ava. "There is never a boring moment."

When Grandma, with Ava close behind her, entered the TV room, Gigi was not happy.

"I don't want 'that dog' near me and she is not coming into this room," she said.

Hearing the angry tone of Gigi's voice, Ava hid behind Grandma.

"She'll behave herself," said Grandma putting a protective hand on Ava's head. "She'll stay by me."

Then she turned to Ava and told her to sit and stay on the floor. Ava obeyed but as soon as Grandma put her head down Ava jumped up on the couch and curled up by her feet. Grandma had no energy for arguments so she let Ava stay. Soon they both dozed off.

When Grandma woke up, her hand and right foot were asleep. She couldn't move because Ava was lying next to her with two paws on her shoulders. Grandma tried to push her off but the dog was big and heavy and not moving until finally roused. It was only then that Grandma was able to get off the couch.

"She better not come near me," said Gigi who had been carefully observing the two.

But Gigi didn't have to worry because Ava was afraid of her and kept a safe distance between them without being told to.

*   *   *

CHAPTER VI

EXPLORING GRANDMA'S HOUSE

Grandma was preparing dinner. Ava who had found comfort lying under the kitchen table got bored and decided to move around. Her curiosity got the best of her and she left to explore the rest of the house. Until now she had only seen the kitchen, the living room, dining room and the TV room which were all on the ground floor. She wondered what else was in the house.

Interesting scents carried her into the hallway and to the stairs where Cuppa had stood when Ava first met this family. Slowly she took the steps one at a time until she got to a landing where there was a large window that looked out into the back yard. Ava rested her paws on the sill. There wasn't a soul outside. No excitement here. She turned and continued up the remaining steps to the second floor.

She stopped at the top and looked around. In the hallway were four doors. They were all open. She decided to try the first one. It was to her right. This door led her into a bright room with a large bed that was covered with a fluffy quilt. It invited her to come and play. Without a doubt this was where Grandma slept because her scent was everywhere. Ava jumped up on the bed and let her body sink into the soft cover. She bounced up and down and rolled around. It was like being on a trampoline. But, as

a child would, Ava soon tired of the game and moved on to something new.

At the far end of Grandma's bedroom Ava saw another door. It beckoned her to come in and explore. As she went inside she saw two steps leading to a bathtub. Streams of sunlight coming through a large window lit up the room. Several potted plants around the bathtub made her feel like she was outdoors. Ava went up the steps and took a whiff of each pot but none of them held any special attraction or magic because no dogs had ever done anything in them. They just smelled like dirt. She wasn't tempted to dig and play.

She next noticed an open door to her left. It was to Grandma's closet. Here Grandma's perfume was so strong it was practically screaming at her but it was mixed with the aroma of soap and cold cream. This was nice. On the floor she spotted a wastebasket into which she stuck her nose and discovered that the scents were especially strong there. The wastebasket was full of Kleenex that Grandma had used to remove her makeup.

Ava couldn't resist pulling out the pieces of soft paper, tearing them and tossing them into the air. She chased them around as they flew about the room. Soon the closet, bathroom and bedroom floor were covered with fine shreds of paper. When the wastebasket was empty, Ava's game was finished so she moved on to something else.

She went back into the hallway where she passed through another door. Here was a smaller bedroom. It was certain that this was Gigi's. Against the wall there was a bed. It also looked inviting so Ava jumped up on it, lay on her back and rolled from left to right rubbing her back on the cover. But Ava miscalculated. This bed was smaller than Grandma's and, not being careful while rolling around, she slipped off the edge and landed on the floor. She let out a small yelp but was back on her feet in seconds. She didn't fall hard and began polishing her claws on the carpeting.

Her attention next went to a wastebasket beside the bed. As she approached it she detected sweet smells coming from it just as she had in Grandma's room. This basket was also full of Kleenex and Ava shredded the contents until no pieces remained. The second floor looked like a snow storm had hit the house. Ava jumped up on Gigi's bed and got comfortable. After all, she needed some rest since she had had so much physical activity. She stretched and yawned. Life was good and, for the moment, Ava forgot about Dad, Spring Break, Grandma and Gigi until she heard Grandma's loud voice calling her.

"Ava!"

*   *   *

.

CHAPTER VII

DINNER TIME

Grandma didn't notice that Ava had left the kitchen. When done with her work she glanced at the clock. It was feeding time for Ava but Ava was nowhere around. Her usual place under the kitchen table was empty and she wasn't resting on the dining room floor. *Where could she be?*

Grandma's heart skipped a beat.

She wasn't sure if the dog would behave in the house. Now she wished she would have let her outside before she started dinner. Cleaning up a mess that Ava might make was not something she looked forward to.

In a panic she shouted, "Ava!"

There was no response.

Where could that dog *have gone?*

Ava had stayed by her side since they became friends. This was not good. So she went searching.

In the hallway there were no signs of her so Grandma automatically went into the room where Gigi was watching TV.

"Have you seen Ava?" she asked Gigi.

"She has not been in here and she better not come near me," said Gigi. "I don't want 'that dog' around."

"I should have known this would be the last place where she would go," mumbled Grandma more to herself.

She took a deep breath. Nothing was going right. It promised to be a long week. She started back toward the kitchen and when she got to the base of the stairs there stood Ava, looking at her with those beautiful, large brown eyes.

"Where have you been?" asked Grandma.

Ava wagged her tail.

"I hope you didn't make a doggie mess that I'll have to clean up."

Ava wagged her tail more.

"It's time for your dinner," said Grandma.

Ava was having so much fun that she forgot all about eating. But on hearing the familiar word DINNER she displayed her happiness by whining and jumping as she had when she heard the word WALK. Grandma laughed.

"You are a silly one," she said forgetting about her anxiety. She headed for the kitchen.

Ava followed and watched as Grandma filled her bowl with dog food. Grandma held it in her hand. Dad had instructed her to tell Ava to sit and shake hands before she gets her food. So Grandma followed Dad's dictates and Ava, obedient and well behaved dog that she was, did exactly as she was told.

"Well, well. I'm impressed," said Grandma. "You are a very smart dog." She rubbed the top of Ava's head.

So having finished with these preliminary exercises, Grandma set the bowl on the floor. But Ava simply stared at it. She didn't touch it.

"What's the matter? Aren't you hungry?" asked Grandma.

Ava fixed her gaze on Grandma but didn't move a muscle.

Grandma was perplexed. She had never met a dog that didn't eat food placed in front of her.

"I hope you aren't sick while Dad is away. I won't know what to do," said Grandma.

But as soon as these words left her lips, one of Dad's comments flashed through her mind.

Ava has been trained not to touch her food until she hears the word OK.

Grandma slapped herself on the forehead.

"Sorry, Puppy," she apologized. Then she added with emphasis. "OK."

The word was barely out of her mouth when Ava attacked the bowl of food as if she hadn't eaten in days. She slurped and gulped and made unappetizing noises until the bowl was empty. It took no more than a minute for her to consume everything that she had been served.

"You couldn't possibly have enjoyed any of that. You ate it much too fast," said Grandma.

Ava licked her chops as if to say thank you. She then looked up at Grandma before settling down comfortably on the kitchen floor.

*   *   *

CHAPTER VIII

BEDTIME

At nine o'clock that evening the family was relaxing in front of the television set. Cuppa had fallen asleep on the couch and Ava was half asleep on the floor by his feet. It had been a long day and Gigi announced that she was ready to go to bed. Because she was old and frail, Grandma helped her up the stairs. Ava perked up and watched the two women as they left the room. Slowly she got up and followed keeping a comfortable distance behind. On reaching the stairs Gigi held tightly to the rail with her left hand and to Grandma with her right. Slowly they took one step at a time.

Ava watched them. Then she followed.

"Get away, dog," said Gigi. She wanted to shoo Ava away with her hands but couldn't let go of the handrail. "Don't you come near me."

"If you ignore her," said Grandma, "she will not bother you. We have to keep moving. She will stay out of the way."

When they reached the upstairs hallway, Grandma noticed some white stuff on the carpeting. They looked like pieces of lint. She didn't think anything about it but made a mental note to pick them up after she got Gigi settled in her room. On stepping into Gigi's room she stopped in her track. The floor was covered in pieces that looked like shredded Kleenex.

"Good grief!" she screamed. "What in heaven's name happened here?" Then she screamed "Ava!" Her voice was loud. "So this is how you entertained yourself while I was in the kitchen."

Ava froze on the spot, tucked her tail between her legs and ran downstairs.

Seeing the mess, Gigi shouted, "He should never have gotten 'that dog' and we should not be taking care of her. She does not belong in this house and she is not coming into my room. From now on I am keeping my door latched."

"Ava!" Grandma again shouted so Ava was sure to hear. "What have you done?"

Ava was terrified. She wasn't sure what she had done that made Grandma carry on so. She wanted to put as much distance as she could between herself and these two women and ran to the kitchen where she curled up under the table.

After getting Gigi settled Grandma started picking up the paper from the floor grumbling all the while.

"Here I am caring for you, feeding you, taking you for walks and this is the thanks I get. I can't believe you could do this to me."

And Grandma didn't stop. As long as she was working she ranted on getting louder by the minute. She didn't quiet down until everything was cleaned up. Ava laid low while she heard Grandma's voice carrying on. She didn't move until it became quiet. Slowly she got up from under the table and cautiously made her way toward the stairs. The turmoil seemed to be over. Ava paused and listened. No sounds. Perhaps now it was safe to go upstairs. Quietly she climbed the steps. There was no one near the landing nor in the upstairs hallway. She peeked into Grandma's bedroom. Grandma was sitting on the bed. She looked up when Ava entered and shook her head.

"What did you do?" she asked sternly.

Ava lowered her head. She didn't know that she had done anything wrong nor did she know why Grandma was so upset.

"You made a mess, puppy," said Grandma. "And I had to clean it all up. Don't ever do that again."

On hearing Grandma's firm tone, Ava kind of understood that her game with the paper was something she should not have done. It sure did make Grandma upset and she was sorry. She tucked in her tail and crouched down on the floor. Slowly she rolled over on her back with her four feet up in the air. It was her way of saying "Sorry."

Grandma looked down at this playful dog lying on her back asking for forgiveness and all her anger was gone.

"Silly dog," she laughed as she patted Ava's tummy. "At least you didn't make a 'doggy mess' that would have been awful to clean up."

Hearing friendly and happy sounds again, Ava rolled over and stood up.

"Don't ever do that again," said Grandma as she shook her finger.

Because of this reprimand Ava rolled on her back again with all fours up in the air.

Grandma laughed. "What am I going to do with you and what have I gotten myself into," she said. "You are going to be quite a challenge. Now let's go downstairs. I want you to go outside one more time before we go to bed."

When Grandma let Ava back into the house, she wanted to lock her up for the night. She said the word KENNEL because she was told that when Ava hears that word she will go right into her cage. After the Kleenex incident, Grandma was not going to let Ava roam around the house during the day or during the night. She wanted Ava in the kennel for sure.

When Ava heard the word KENNEL she sat on the kitchen floor as if she didn't hear or understand what Grandma was saying. Grandma stood by the cage and called and signaled but Ava ignored her.

"You understood OK when I fed you and you understood WALK and DINNER, why don't you understand KENNEL when it's bedtime?" asked Grandma. "I think you're testing me."

Grandma pulled Ava by the collar and led her to the cage.

Ava followed Grandma's lead quietly. She sniffed the familiar things from home, her toys, pillow and her blanket. The smells reminded her of Dad and she felt content. She made herself comfortable.

Grandma closed the kennel door and said good night. It then hit her that in the few hours that she and Ava had spent together a bond had grown between them. She didn't see Ava as a Pit Bull any more but as a young child who needed love and care.

*   *   *

CHAPTER IX

THE FIRST MORNING

Thre was a chill in the air and total darkness filled the bedroom when the shrill of the alarm clock shook the sleep from Grandma's eyes. She shuddered as she pulled her arm from under the covers. In trying to reach the clock she managed to push it farther from her reach. The sound now was deafening, as if a hundred off-key trumpets were blaring into her ears. She gritted her teeth and propped herself on her elbows. The clock was at the far end of the nightstand and the brightly illuminated numbers showed 6:35. It had been ringing since 6:30.

"Oh no," groaned Grandma. "I don't want to get up." She pulled the clock closer to her and pushed the button.

A peaceful quiet enveloped the room. It was nice. Grandma sighed as she dropped her head back onto the pillow. She could hardly believe that the thing was ringing for almost five minutes before she heard it. It was so tempting to roll over, pull up the covers and go back to sleep but it was a work day and she had to get up. A vision of the dog, entrusted to her care, flashed in her mind. *Oh no,* she groaned. She also had to take care of Ava.

Crawling out of bed into a cold, dark room had to be the nastiest experience in the whole wide world. Grandma turned on the bedside lamp. Harsh yellow light flooded the room and burned her eyes. She squeezed her eyelids shut for protection. A few seconds later she could open them without pain. She then dragged herself out of bed, got dressed and went downstairs.

"Good morning," she said as she approached her guest. Ava appeared comfortable in the kennel. She was wagging her tail and seemed happy to see Grandma – or so Grandma thought. Actually Ava had had enough of being locked up and was ready to get out. When Grandma opened the door to the kennel she led Ava to the back door and into the yard. It was dark outside but not quiet.

Grandma's house was on the corner and movement on the sidewalk and the street could be easily heard. There were sounds from cars and buses driving past which were of no interest to Ava. But the voices of joggers which traveled in the quiet darkness bothered her. She didn't like the fact that she couldn't see who was speaking. So she began barking.

"Hush," said Grandma opening the door. "People are still sleeping. We can't disturb them."

Ava ran inside not understanding what was going on. She sat on the kitchen floor and, while she waited to be fed, Grandma started to make breakfast for herself and Gigi but not Cuppa. He had quietly slipped out of the house while Grandma was still in dreamland. There was no one to assist her with the dog or with Gigi.

When she finished making breakfast she went up to help Gigi down the stairs. And while the two women had their coffee and toast Ava sat patiently waiting.

Grandma was in deep thought. What to do with Ava while she was at work had gnawed at her last night before she was able to fall asleep. If she left her at home, Ava would be in the kennel all day. Grandma could never do that to her. Besides, leaving her alone in the house with Gigi was completely out of the question. After several hours of tossing and turning she decided to take Ava to work with her. Then and only then was she able to relax and fall into a deep slumber.

Morning came very soon, though, and now she wondered if she had made the right decision. She looked at Ava who was sitting near her bowl patiently waiting for her breakfast. When Ava saw Grandma look at her she came over and put her chin on Grandma's lap.

"I didn't forget you," said Grandma patting Ava's head. She got up to fill her bowl and gave the commands, SIT and SHAKE, before she set the full bowl on the floor then gave the magic word, OK, after the bowl was on the floor.

Grandma watched Ava attack the dish and wondered if the people at work would want to spend their day with this big brown dog. It was not a promising picture but that's the way it was.

Grandma put her coffee cup in the dishwasher and snapped Ava's leash to her collar. The two of them stepped out the back door. The day was overcast and gloomy. Thick clouds blocked the smiling face of the sun and the sweet chirping of the birds was nowhere to be

heard. This was a bad omen. It was going to be a long day and an even longer week.

In the driveway Grandma opened the back door of the car and Ava climbed in. While Grandma went around to the driver's side, Ava jumped into the front passenger seat.

"You can't sit there," said Grandma.

Ava stared at her as if she didn't understand.

"Get in the back," said Grandma using a more firm tone as she got into the car.

Ava didn't move but looked at Grandma with her big, sad, brown eyes. Grandma was tired and irritable and she was beginning to lose her patience.

"I do not understand why you like to ignore me," said Grandma. "Sometimes I feel like I'm talking to the wall. You're just like a disobedient child. I thought dogs are always supposed to do what humans say."

Ava stared at Grandma and she appeared to not understand the words that were directed at her. Then looking as if offended, she lowered her head. Still she didn't move.

Grandma felt guilty that she was talking this way to this "fatherless child" who had been left in her care and who was probably terribly homesick.

"OK," she said as she pulled Ava by the collar to coax her into the back seat. Ava slowly moved and got settled behind Grandma.

"You have to stay in the back so you don't get hurt," said Grandma.

*   *   *

CHAPTER X

AT GRANDMA'S WORK

It was lonely in the back seat but Ava was quiet because Grandma's voice had meant business. As she sat up straight and looked out the window she saw things she had never seen before: pedestrians walking their dogs, people on bicycles, big houses and lots of businesses. A long time later, or so it seemed to Ava, Grandma pulled into a parking lot in front of a two story brick building.

They got out of the car. Ava was intrigued by all the new scents and wanted to sniff around but Grandma was not stopping for anything until she got to the building.

The front door led them into an alcove with cinder block walls on each side. Facing them was a glass wall with a wooden door in the center. The door was locked.

While Grandma was turning keys on her key ring looking for the one to unlock the door, Ava saw two people in the office on the other side of the glass wall. It looked like they were talking to each other. When they heard Grandma's key in the lock they looked up and saw Ava's face through the glass. They didn't come to the door to help open it nor did they step up to greet Grandma. They quickly left the room. Because Grandma was behind the wooden door she had not seen the two people and, when she finally got inside, there was no one around.

The ringing of the telephone interrupted their entrance. Grandma hurried to the big desk in the center of the office and sat down to pick up the phone. She dropped Ava's leash as she became immersed in her conversation, busily taking notes on a piece of paper as she spoke. She didn't notice that Ava left her side.

Ava was free to roam. As usual, her curiosity got the best of her and she was ready to see what else there was in this large building in addition to the front office. Grandma hadn't let her sniff the yard, the parking lot or any part outside the building. She missed out on all that which is considered fun for dogs. But now she felt her freedom and could do whatever she wanted.

Dragging her leash behind her Ava wandered away. New and enticing odors led her through an open door to a large room where she saw two people working by some big instruments. They had not noticed her come in. One of them, a skinny man with thick, wire rimmed glasses that had slipped down his nose, had his back to her. He was concentrating on a computer monitor when Ava

approached him. Quietly she rubbed her nose against his arm as she breathed in his scent. This skinny man, surprised by the unfamiliar contact to his body, instinctively jerked away and with his index finger pushed his glasses further up his nose to see more clearly what was touching him. He gasped when he saw Ava and slowly stood up from his chair. With his arms lifted into the air as if someone was holding a gun to his chest he backed out of the room through a door on the opposite wall.

The other person, an equally studious looking man but on the heavier side and wearing horn rimmed glasses, was sitting at another instrument several feet away. Being totally immersed in his work, he had not noticed his colleague's departure. As Ava approached him, he caught from the corner of his eye, her brown color. He instinctively jerked away but looked to get a clearer view. Startled by her closeness and her appearance, he hoped to get away. But he didn't want to create a ruckus nor cause any movement that might agitate this scary looking dog. Very slowly he stood up from his chair. His heart was beating rapidly and his breathing was heavy. He stepped away from his workstation and walked backwards out of the room never taking his eyes off Ava.

Ava wanted to befriend these two people as she did most humans but she was soon distracted by wonderful new scents. It was an old building and had a history of many years behind it. Moving her nose along the floor while sniffing every inch, she reached a wall. She paused and looked around. This was just short of heaven.

She was jolted from her entertainment by Grandma's familiar and loud voice coming from the front office.

"Ava!"

Grandma panicked. She had finished her conversation and saw that Ava was not near her.

Not again, she thought. Visions of Ava shredding paper from the wastebaskets in the building were dancing through her mind. The thought of cleaning up after her put a shiver down her back.

"Ava, come," she called even louder, sounding frantic.

When Ava heard her she came bounding in.

"Where have you been, Puppy, and where is everyone?" she said as she picked up the leash. "You can't be running around here."

Grandma intended to slowly introduce Ava to those who worked there hoping that they would like her and accept her presence. She didn't know that Ava had already met two people. So she went into the big instrument room looking for the employees. There wasn't a person in sight. And there were people in the building. That was sure. Their cars were in the parking lot. Grandma scratched her head. It was perplexing. She continued to the door through which the two people had disappeared. There she found them and two others. They were standing in a corner.

"Good morning," said Grandma.

They stared at her, eyes wide open, fear on their faces. No one said a word.

Ava started toward them but Grandma held her on a short leash. Grandma sighed deeply. Yes, it was going to be a very long day. Obviously everyone at work was terrified of her. Overwhelmed with frustration and weary from a sleepless night Grandma turned on her heel and led Ava back to the front office where she sat down at the desk to think.

Ava sat on the floor by Grandma's feet and looked up at her with those big brown eyes. Grandma felt a lump in her throat as she patted Ava gently on her head.

Now what. She was ready to cry when the sound of rattling keys made her look toward the front door. Ava picked up her ears. Another person was coming in to work It was a perky, young blonde, who greeted Grandma with a cheerful hello as she skipped inside.

"Good morning," answered Grandma trying to sound happy.

When the blonde came around the desk and saw Ava sitting by Grandma's feet she stopped dead in her tracks.

"Wha...wha...what is that?" she stammered, her perk completely gone.

"Oh, my gosh," replied Grandma with more than a little irritation in her voice. "It's a dog."

The blonde was in a state of shock unable to move but still able to stammer when she realized that Grandma was holding tightly to Ava's leash.

"I kn know it's a dog, but it's a Pit Bull," she finally spit it out.

"A dog is a dog. It has four legs and since the dawn of time, I have been told," said Grandma, "it has been known as man's best friend."

But the blonde was not convinced that this creature could possibly be a friend to anything or anybody. Keeping as far away as the room allowed without banging into the wall or tripping on furniture, she quickly made her way toward the big instrument room taking her eyes off Ava only when she was safely out of the front office.

To avoid an encounter with anyone else, Grandma went upstairs to her own office and closed the door behind her. She unclipped Ava's leash.

"You can move around in here as you wish but it looks like we are stuck for the day. I'll take you outside later."

While Grandma worked at her desk Ava stayed on the floor. The day dragged. After a few hours Ava was ready to do something. She went over to Grandma and put her head on her lap. Ava's big brown eyes showed boredom and a need for a change of scenery.

"I'm ready to take a break too," said Grandma to Ava. She stroked the dog's head then stood up and stretched.

It had been two hours since she had sat in her chair and had gotten stiff and sore. Then checking the time she saw that it was still early for the lunch crowd to be eating. If she hurried, she could beat them to the break room.

With Ava secure on her leash, Grandma got downstairs without running into anyone. In the lunchroom she found a bowl and filled it with water. The poor dog, who by this time was parched, slurped up the contents and created a sloppy mess on the floor.

"That wasn't very lady like," commented Grandma, as she wiped up the splatter.

Ava looked innocently up at her.

"OK, I didn't mean it. I know it hasn't been fun sitting upstairs. I'm sorry."

Grandma took her lunch bag with her and went outside. In the parking lot she munched on a cheese sandwich as she and Ava walked around the grounds that surrounded the building. It was a slow and leisurely stroll because Ava stopped to smell everything that was out there. And both dog and human were relaxed for the first time since they started their day, Ava because she was allowed to sniff whatever she wanted and Grandma because she was at peace with her surroundings.

The morning clouds had disappeared and the sun was a bright golden ball up above. Other than the sound of a few cars slowly passing by, it was quiet all around them. The fresh air was soothing. Grandma didn't want to go back into the building. She wanted to stay outside for the rest of the day and not have to face anyone again. But that could not be.

When they came back inside the two men whom Ava had met earlier, the blonde and several other people were in the front office. This time they didn't hide or run away. They felt safe because of their numbers. Furthermore, the dog was not aggressive or loud. She didn't growl or show her teeth and had not taken a taste of Grandma during the time they had spent in the building. They came to the conclusion that their own lives were not in danger. Besides, Grandma was holding tightly to the leash.

They started asking questions about the dog, how Grandma had managed to get her and was she going to be coming to work on a regular basis.

Grandma told them about the shelter and about Dad and politely answered all their questions. During this time Ava sat quietly by Grandma's feet.

The skinny man with the thick glasses came closer and let Ava smell his hands but then stepped away. He didn't want any more contact with her than that. The others were more cautious and kept a safe distance.

It looked like the air in the building had eased and that some of the stress from the employees toward the dog was lifted. But it was not good to push it. Tomorrow was another day and Ava was here for the entire week. There was plenty of time to further develop the friendships between the two species. Grandma and Ava went back upstairs to her office and stayed there until it was time to go home.

*　　*　　*

CHAPTER XI

MAKING FRIENDS WITH GIGI

The big clock on the office wall showed five. *Thank goodness this day is done*, thought Grandma, sighing deeply. Finally it was time to go home. She clipped the leash on Ava and led her downstairs. Outside she let Ava take as much time as she wanted on that short distance between building and vehicle. Although Ava had sniffed everything during lunchtime, she couldn't get enough of all the wonderful odors. She took her time to go over the unfamiliar terrain and relish it all. And Grandma was in no hurry. She let her do as she wanted.

"What more is there to smell?" asked Grandma laughing. "Nothing new happened this afternoon."

Ava took no notice of her. She was enjoying herself.

When they reached the car, Grandma opened the door. Ava got into the back seat without any prompting and stayed there. She was happy.

The drive home was quiet with traffic unusually light for that time of the day. It was actually relaxing with the sun shining in through the windows and soft music playing on the radio. It was almost too good.

Then a thought flashed in Grandma's mind: *Gigi.* Getting closer to home, Grandma's heart rate got faster and small beads of perspiration formed along the hairline on her forehead. Her stomach was queasy as she pulled into the driveway.

Why can't things be easier? She thought to herself.

Gigi was sitting at the kitchen table. She had been looking out the window waiting for Grandma to come home. She greeted Grandma but ignored Ava. She did give Ava a look, though, to let her know she didn't want her around. Ava got the message. She stayed away from Gigi. So while the two women sat down to a quiet dinner that Gigi had cooked, Ava curled up on the rug in the dining room. She kept her eyes half open, half shut as she listened to the women converse.

Gigi talked about the daily news that she had watched on TV and asked Grandma how her day had gone.

Grandma sighed. "Everyone at work was afraid of her. We stayed locked in my office all day."

"As I said before," said Gigi, "he should have never gotten 'that dog'."

"That's fine," answered Grandma, "but he did and I told him I would dog sit. Nothing can be done about it now."

Since Gigi's voice was not as harsh as during their previous encounters, Ava felt brave and came into the kitchen. She moved closer to Gigi but Gigi immediately put a stop to that.

"Do not come near me," she said gritting her teeth, sounding as she had in the past.

Ava backed away. She didn't have to be told twice. She didn't understand why Gigi didn't like her.

The fact was that Gigi had heard awful stories about Pit Bulls and how they had mauled people. She didn't trust her and was afraid of her. So Ava went back into the other room watching through the doorway until Gigi left the kitchen and Grandma called her for dinner.

After Ava slurped down her food Grandma took her for a quick walk around the block. Luckily they didn't encounter any frightened pedestrians or stray dogs.

"How can I be so lucky," said Grandma when they got back. She patted Ava's head.

It had been a long day and Grandma was tired. She stretched out on the couch in front of the television set. She was relaxed in the familiar atmosphere of her home. Her eyes were heavy and she was barely able to keep them open. Ava curled up on the floor by her feet. But she wasn't relaxed. There was Gigi keeping a sharp eye on her.

Eventually Ava did close her eyes until Gigi sneezed and disturbed the quiet of the evening. Ava, startled by the noise, jumped to her feet. She went nearer to Gigi. For a moment their eyes met and Gigi could see into Ava's big brown eyes. She felt a warmth rush through her body. It was strange.

The dog no longer looked like the vicious attack dog she saw earlier. Instead she now saw loyalty and love. Staring into Ava's eyes Gigi saw the warm heart that lay within that innocent creature. She didn't touch Ava but smiled at her. It was as if a fine electrical current passed between them.

Yes, it is the eyes that show what is inside the heart whether it's human or man's best friend. Someone who cannot look another in the eye has something to hide. Whether it's evil, pain, sorrow or love, it can be seen and recognized by others because the heart is visible through the eyes. And Gigi saw that inside Ava was a sweet and loving creature.

Grandma did not see the exchange between her mother and the pet because she was sound asleep.

*   *   *

CHAPTER XII

ANOTHER DAY AT WORK

Grandma slept well during the night but when she awoke she was irritable. The morning rituals went the same as the previous day and when Grandma opened the back door of the car, Ava stepped in. By the time Grandma got to the driver's side, Ava was comfortably seated behind the steering wheel.

"We have to set some rules here," said Grandma. "I drive and you stay in the back seat."

Ava stared as if she didn't understand. Grandma gave her a nudge. Ava got the message but took her time going into the back.

The arrival at work went smoothly because they were greeted by the employees who had already met Ava.

But not everyone had met her. And to prevent any unpleasant encounters, Grandma did stay in her office as much as she could. She made occasional visits downstairs, though, and the few people that were meeting Ava for the first time seemed to be more open to her presence.

Lunchtime was again spent walking around the parking lot and the yard. It was probably the most relaxing part of the day.

After lunch, though, when Grandma came back into the building, the phone was ringing in the front office. Because no one was at the big desk she answered it. Momentarily she dropped the leash as she grabbed a pen and paper to take notes. Had anyone been watching her they would have let off sirens warning her to pay heed. But, alas, there was no one around and no alarm blaring. And Ava once again was set free and soon out of sight.

When Ava felt her leash slacken she slowly wandered off. After all, that place had the most wonderful smells that she had ever come across. She was happy but there was one problem. Not everyone that she encountered during her explorations was pleased to see her. Among them was a man that she had not met before.

When Grandma finished with the phone call she looked about. Ava was not by her side. Her head started to throb as she thought of what she would find as she went looking for the dog. Stepping into the big room where everyone was working, she saw Ava standing near a tall, dark haired man who during the past two days had been absent from work. Grandma said hello to him and asked how he was. She then went over to Ava and picked up her leash. The man didn't respond. He only glared at Grandma. His face was beet red showing both anger and fear at the same time. He bared his teeth, squinted his eyes and began in a frightful tone of voice.

"I don't want your dog to touch me and I don't want her anywhere near me," he screamed viciously and stormed out of the room.

Grandma was speechless. She had no idea that that person had felt so strongly and had such dislike for the dog. It seemed that most people had made friends with Ava and were willing to accept her on the premises. This outburst came as a shock. It wounded Grandma deeply. She led Ava upstairs and they stayed there until it was time to go home.

Interestingly, Ava was not bothered by the man's outburst. In fact, she barely noticed him because she so enjoyed the building.

*   *   *

CHAPTER XIII

AVA STAYS HOME WITH GIGI

That evening Grandma was unusually quiet. She didn't speak during dinner but thought long and hard. After the last incident in the office, she came to the conclusion that she could not take Ava to work with her any more. It was too difficult to deal with the employees and their fear of the dog.

Next morning as she sat at the table picking at her breakfast, her heart was heavy.

Finally she said to Gigi. "I will put Ava in the kennel and I'll drive home during lunchtime to let her out."

Ava sensed that something was different. She put her head on Grandma's lap. Grandma patted her head, smiled but didn't say anything more.

Ava anticipated the day at work with Grandma. She was a smart dog and picked up habits quickly. She was ready for the long ride which was followed by the stay in the large building. So while Grandma went upstairs to do what she did to get ready, Ava waited by the back door. It seemed forever until she heard Grandma's footsteps coming down the stairs. Ava perked up. She was ready to leave. But Grandma didn't come. Instead she was calling from the other room.

"Come, Ava, come," she said. "Kennel."

This was confusing and not part of their routine. Ava had spent the night in the kennel and was not ready to go back in. Besides she was looking forward to the car ride.

She held fast to her post by the door but Grandma persisted. It was a stalemate. No one was moving. Unless one of them gave in they would stay in the same position for a long time.

Then Grandma was quiet. She quit calling. Perhaps she had given up. Ava stood up ready to go out the door when a cross looking Grandma loomed over her. The stress from the last few days was written all over her face.

"I will be late for work. Get into the kennel NOW," she growled and grabbed Ava by the collar.

Grandma had never spoken to her so harshly not even when she created the snow storm upstairs. Not understanding what could have triggered this angry outburst Ava lowered her head. She rolled over on her back with all fours up in the air. She wanted to let Grandma know that she was sorry for whatever she may have done.

"Don't play games with me," shouted Grandma. "Get up."

Ava's world was crumbling. Very slowly she stood up and, with her head down, went where Grandma was pulling her. She was about to cry and wished that Dad was back.

Seeing the dejected look on Ava's face, Grandma regretted having been so harsh and spoke softly. "I am so sorry, Puppy. I hate to do this to you but I cannot take you to work. I'll be back at lunchtime. Until then you be good." With that she latched the kennel door and left.

Ava buried her nose in her blanket. There she found comfort in the familiar smells. It calmed her. Yet it was troubling not to know what she had done to make Grandma so upset. To add to her misery she got a whiff of Gigi's scent. She shuddered. To be left alone with Gigi was a nightmare. What more could happen to make her life worse?

Cautiously she looked around but couldn't see anything. It was obvious that Gigi was close but she was not in her line of vision. She had to rely on her sense of hearing and smell. Judging from the scraping sounds on the floor Ava figured that Gigi had pulled out the chair and was sitting by the kitchen table. Other than the blaring of the television there were no other sounds until the telephone rang. This was followed by Gigi's walker clanking across the floor. When Gigi stopped so did the ringing of the phone.

"Hello," said Gigi as she answered. She continued speaking. A few minutes later it was quiet. Gigi then left the kitchen and went in the direction of the TV room. The sound of Gigi's walker slowly drifted off until all was quiet. Burying her nose in her blanket Ava dozed off. She woke to the now familiar sounds of Gigi's movements. The lady was coming in her direction. Ava's heart beat faster. Gigi was getting close. Then she heard her voice.

"What have you been doing? Are you comfortable?"

It startled Ava. She looked up. There was Gigi standing by the cage. She didn't know what this woman wanted and hoped she would leave. She put her head back down.

"Do you want to go outside?" asked Gigi.

Ava lifted her head. Of course she was ready to go outside. She had spent the night and most of the morning in the kennel. Yes, she wanted to go out. She wanted to move and stretch and run around. It had been a long time since she was free. She moved her tail back and forth. Gigi reached down and unlatched the kennel door. She then shuffled to the kitchen and opened the back door. Ava at first hesitated, not sure if she wanted to follow Gigi or be near her. She had mixed feelings. If she wanted to go outside, though, she had to pass by Gigi. As she approached the door, she picked up her pace and rushed past Gigi and outside.

When the fresh air hit her face, Ava was happy. She ran down the steps and around the small enclosure which

they called the back yard. It took several rounds about the perimeter before she found just the right spot to relieve herself. She then stretched all her limbs and comfortably lay down in a patch of sunshine that was warming the concrete. It was nice to be outside.

Ava was loving every minute until Gigi's voice came from behind the screen door. "What are you doing lying down? I thought you'd be glad to get out and run around. I've never seen a dog like you. Why aren't you moving and getting a little exercise?"

Ava turned her head toward the door but otherwise gave no response. Her face showed no emotion although she was happy just the way she was. She made no movement toward Gigi or the door.

"Do you want to come inside?" asked Gigi. But Ava looked away from her pretending that she didn't hear. "Suit yourself," said Gigi, shrugging her shoulders. She shut the door.

It seemed like no time at all when Gigi was back. "Have you had enough? Are you ready to come in after all your heavy exercise?"

Ava didn't catch the sarcasm in Gigi's voice.

"Come inside," prompted Gigi.

Ava stood up and stretched. It looked like Gigi wasn't going to leave her alone as long as she stayed outside. Slowly she started toward the door. She took the steps one at a time and stopped when she reached the top. She looked up at Gigi who was holding open the door. Ava paused for a moment then rushed past Gigi and straight to the kennel. Gigi closed the back door and slowly followed Ava's path. When she got to the kennel she latched the door.

"I thought you're supposed to be a scary and vicious dog," said Gigi. "It looks like you're nothing but a sissy."

Ava turned her head away.

"Hmph," said Gigi. "And it looks like you don't have good manners. You're supposed to look at me when I'm talking to you."

Ava ignored her.

With that Gigi trudged off toward the TV room and all was quiet once again.

*   *   *

CHAPTER XIV

GRANDMA AT WORK ALONE

That morning when Grandma arrived at work everything played out as usual. Grandma unlocked the door. The phone rang. She sat at the big desk and answered it. She took notes and when she hung up Blondie was coming in at the front door. She was perky as usual and when she came around she looked for Ava.

"Where is your dog?" she asked.

"I didn't bring her," was all that Grandma said. She got up from the desk and went upstairs to her office. She was miserable.

Later she came down to take a break. Everybody that ran into her asked about Ava, everybody except the one angry man who had screamed at her the day before.

Fortunately he was nowhere around. Grandma didn't know what she would say to him if she did see him.

Now it was nearing lunchtime and there was a lull in her day. The phone was quiet for the moment and Grandma had caught up with her paperwork. She was ready for a break. Standing up from her chair she stretched her back and arms. Her eyes drifted to the spot where Ava would rest while they were in the office together. There was no one there.

Visions of the dog flashed in her mind and her heart was filled with guilt and remorse. She missed Ava and felt miserable as she re-lived the scenes from earlier that morning. She couldn't shake them from her mind. Every time she finished working on something she thought of Ava. She had been too hard on her. It wasn't Ava's fault that Grandma didn't get enough sleep and that she was stressed out. Poor thing couldn't help the response and reaction of others to her breed. But Pit Bulls had a bad reputation. People responded the way they did because of it. Even Grandma had reacted to Ava negatively when she first met her. It was a fact of life and there was nothing she could do about it. But taking it out on the dog was not right and the guilt didn't leave her.

I'll make it up to her when I get home, she thought.

Grandma looked at the big clock on the wall. She would have to leave in a few minutes. Her plans for the day were circling in her mind. She would leave around lunch time, eat her sandwich in the car then let Ava out for a little romp in the back yard. She would come back to work for the afternoon. It was perfect. It did involve a lot of driving but that's the best solution that she could find.

As these thought played through her mind the telephone rang. Grandma answered. She had to leave in a few minutes and hoped this call wouldn't take long. When she picked up she heard Gigi's voice.

"You don't have to come home. I already let her out. She's fine. Enjoy your day. I'll have dinner ready for you after work." And with that she hung up the phone.

Grandma held on to the earpiece long after the call disconnected and stood frozen. It took several minutes for Gigi's words to sink in. She put the receiver down. It felt like someone had taken a two ton brick off her shoulders.

But she had questions, thousands of them. She wanted to call Gigi back and ask her what had happened but things got busy and she didn't have time. She didn't even notice how fast the day passed until she looked at the clock. It was the end of the work day and time to leave.

The ride home was slow. Thoughts of Ava filled Grandma's mind. She could not even guess what had happened between the two.

*   *   *

CHAPTER XV

SPENDING TIME WITH GIGI

Ava was waiting in the back yard when Grandma got home.

"Who let you out?" she asked as she rubbed Ava's head. Ava wagged her tail and nuzzled up to Grandma. She was happy to see her and followed her into the house.

Inside Gigi was sitting at the kitchen table.

"Was Ava good today?" asked Grandma.

"Yes," replied Gigi. "But she is very quiet. All she does is sleep all day. She even slept when she was out in the back yard."

Grandma didn't ask more questions. If Gigi didn't want to tell her what happened, then she wasn't going to probe. Whatever it was, it was good. She left it at that.

Then, looking at Ava, she said, "You are a good dog." She patted her head.

When they went into the TV room Grandma sat on the couch. Ava tried to climb onto her lap. She wanted to get as close as she could to Grandma. The morning altercation was long forgotten.

"No, Ava. You're too big to be a lap dog. Down." Then turning to Gigi she said, "I have to go to a meeting tonight. Is it all right if I leave Ava out of the kennel while I am gone?"

"It won't bother me," answered Gigi.

Interesting, thought Grandma. *Hmm. What could have happened? But, no, it's best not to ask questions about a good thing.*

Turning to Ava she said, "You be good while I'm gone." She got up and Ava walked her to the door.

The door closed and Ava was alone in the kitchen but not for long. Gigi was coming to get a drink of water. Although Gigi has been using a nicer tone with her, Ava moved out of the way. She headed for the TV room and jumped up on the couch. The couch was OK but she couldn't get comfortable. So she tried Gigi's chair. It was perfect and just the right softness. She curled up and closed her eyes until she heard the clomping of Gigi's walker across the floor. It was coming in her direction.

"What are you doing in my chair?" asked Gigi. Her voice wasn't loud or unpleasant but firm. "Get off. I don't like you on the furniture, especially not on my chair. It's mine and I don't share it with a dog."

Ava jumped off to make way for Gigi. She was a good dog and most of the time obeyed her humans. But she really liked that chair and wasn't happy about having to give it up. She got off, though, then stepped back and watched Gigi. The old lady parked her walker. She then got situated in her chair and wrapped a blanket over her lap. There was nothing for Ava to do but try the other chair that was just like Gigi's. She jumped up on it and curled up. The chair looked the same but it wasn't. She'd keep an eye on Gigi and the minute she got up to leave the room, Ava would be ready to claim that chair for herself.

It was quiet in the room except for the television set's low tones in the background. Both were resting quietly when Gigi began speaking.

"When I was a child we never had animals in the house. My father would not allow it. We lived in the city and didn't have a yard for animals to play. Besides, animals have all kinds of bacteria and aren't clean. So even if we did have a yard we would not have had an animal. Actually, you," and she pointed at Ava, "should not be on the furniture. I don't know why they let you get up on that chair or on the couch. You shouldn't even be in the house. It's unsanitary. And those children (referring to Dad's kids) never wash their hands after they touch you. It's terrible how lax the world has become."

Ava didn't understand a word Gigi was saying but her calm tone sounded good.

"I had a kitten once," she continued. "I was very young at the time, just a little girl. A friend brought it for me. The kitty was small and I could hold her in the palm of my hand. Her whole body was soft and when I touched the little pads of her paws they felt like velvet. To make her look pretty I put a red ribbon around her neck. She purred when I held her. And she was clean. Cats are always washing themselves, you know. They're not like you. But I still couldn't keep her. My father made me give it back to my friend."

Gigi then was quiet. She remembered those days from a long, long time ago. It was another world when she was a little girl surrounded by all different people.

Ava got off the chair and put her head on Gigi's lap. Gigi gently stroked her head and the two stayed like that until the phone rang and disturbed them.

"Now I have to wash my hands," sighed Gigi as she picked up the receiver.

"Hello," she said.

A recorded message was at the other end of the line. Annoyed by the call, Gigi pushed the disconnect button and put the phone down. Slowly she stood up and with her walker went to the bathroom to wash her hands.

Ava was in her chair as soon as she turned her back.

*   *   *

CHAPTER XVI

DAD RETURNS

In the morning Ava waited by the door with tail wagging ready to go to work with Grandma. Grandma patted her head and smiled at her. Without irritation in her voice she said, "Unfortunately, Puppy, your working days are over. You will have to stay home again." She signaled with her hand and said, "Into the kennel." Ava quietly obeyed.

Gigi sat at the kitchen table watching and listening. "You don't have to come home at lunchtime. I'll take care of her."

"Thank you," said Grandma and with a sigh of relief she left.

As soon as the door closed behind her, Gigi got up and shuffled over to the kennel. She lifted the lock and opened the door.

"You can come out. It's not necessary for you to be cooped up all day."

The two ambled into the TV room. Gigi was pushing her walker and Ava was at her heels. Gigi sat in her chair and Ava jumped up on the other. Soon both were asleep, making discordant sounds that would rival a symphony orchestra's warmup session. But it was heard by no one.

The ringing of the telephone woke them. It was Gigi's friend calling. Gigi told her about Ava.

"It's unfortunate that she is not a pretty dog. Actually you could almost say she is ugly. She's large and her face and jowls are huge. But she has a certain charm and warmth about her. She is very lovable and after you get to know her she seems quite beautiful. It's the strangest thing."

When she finished with her conversation, she took her walker and went to the kitchen. Ava followed.

"It's time for you to go outside," said Gigi as she opened the back door. "Take your time and enjoy the fresh air and sunshine."

Ava ran down the steps and around the yard a couple of times before settling down in a spot of sunshine. It was a beautiful day and life was good.

The two spent several quiet days together. Gigi spoke to Ava as if they were long-time friends. Ava had no idea what she was saying but could tell by her demeanor and her tone that it was all good.

As the week was winding down Ava and Gigi were in the kitchen when Grandma arrived home from work. Grandma sat at the kitchen table and Ava put her head in Grandma's lap. Gently Grandma stroked Ava's back. In a quiet voice she said, "Your Dad will be coming shortly to take you home, little dog. They are back from their vacation. I will miss you." There was a lump in her throat and she couldn't say any more.

Gigi took a deep breath. She had made friends with this dog and it was nice having her around these last couple of days. She liked her company and enjoyed not being alone all day.

The two women were quietly pondering Ava's departure, when all of a sudden Ava jumped up and started whining. She became agitated and ran around in circles.

"What's wrong, Puppy, do you have to go outside?" asked Grandma as she opened the door.

Ava went wild. She practically flew off the porch skipping all five steps, whining then jumping into the air. Dad was coming in the gate.

"I guess she's happy to see you," laughed Grandma. She couldn't get close to Dad to give him a hug.

Cody was following behind Dad. He came to help take Ava home. He went inside and found Gigi sitting by the table.

"How did you get along with Ava?" Cody asked Gigi.

"We got along fine. I think I'm going to miss her. She is quite special and very lovable," she answered.

"She can come over and visit you whenever you like," Cody assured her.

Ava and her things were loaded up and Cody and Dad climbed into the truck. Grandma and Gigi stood by the fence and waved as the truck pulled out of the driveway. There was an emptiness in the pit of Grandma's stomach.

"I'm sure she'll be back," she said, "but I will miss her.

"I will too," said Gigi. She wiped a tear from her eye.

* * *

CHAPTER XVII

THE END

Ava did come back many times and they had wonderful visits over the years. Grandma and Gigi loved her companionship and looked forward to having her stay with them. Ava became one of the family and was treated as one of the grandchildren.

Then one autumn afternoon several years after that eventful Spring Break when they all became friends something changed.

Grandma was sitting at the kitchen table working on a crossword puzzle when the phone rang. On the caller ID it had Dad's name.

"Hi," said Grandma, eager to hear her son's voice but there was no sound on the other end of the receiver.

"Hello," she said a bit louder. "Are you there?"

There was a cough, a pause, then came Dad's voice. "I …um." Again a cough. "I …um." Then a pause and a deep breath. Finally his words came across the line. "I have to take Ava to the veterinarian." His voice broke.

Grandma felt a lump in her throat. "

"What's wrong?" She asked. She could hear Dad trying to choke back tears.

"She is very sick and there is nothing they can do to help her. I can't talk anymore."

The line disconnected and the dial tone buzzed loudly in Grandma's ear. Her tears began to flow down her cheeks as she went to tell Gigi.

Grandma and Gigi never saw her again.

Dad had a hard time recovering and after two weeks couldn't deal with the emptiness of losing Ava any more. He visited the shelter and brought home Nina, another pit bull. But Nina never fully replaced Ava. It took a while for Grandma and Gigi to get used to her. The opening scenes with the introductions replayed as previously but somehow it just wasn't the same.

Eventually they learned to love her but in a different way. Ava's memory forever remained in their hearts.

.

.

AUTHOR

After managing a chemistry laboratory for over thirty years Marianne Shrader took up the pen and pursued her love of writing. For the first half of her education she attended Northwestern University and completed her studies at Wayne State University where she majored in foreign languages and minored in chemistry. She currently resides in Michigan with her husband.

Made in the USA
Monee, IL
02 January 2021